A MAZE ADVENTURE

Search for Pirate Treasure

National Geographic would like to thank Claire Schen, Associate Professor of History at the University at Buffalo, The State University of New York, for her expert assistance in reviewing the text in *Search for Pirate Treasure*.

Created and produced by Firecrest Books Ltd
in association with Graham White

First American Edition 2009
Published by the National Geographic Society.

For information about special discounts for bulk purchases, please contact
National Geographic Books Special Sales: ngspecsales@ngs.org

For rights or permissions inquires, please contact
National Geographic Books Subsidiary Rights: ngbookrights@ngs.org

Prepared for the National Geographic Society by Firecrest Books Ltd.

The art was created by Graham White on computer with watercolor software.
Book design by Phil Jacobs
The body text of the book is set in Galliard.

Library of Congress Catalog-in-Publication Data:
Available upon request

ISBN: 978-1-4263-0459-0

Founded in 1888, the National Geographic Society is one of the largest scientific and educational organizations in the world. It reaches more than 285 million people worldwide each month through its official journal, NATIONAL GEOGRAPHIC, and its four other magazines; The National Geographic Channel; television documentaries; radio programs; films; books; videos and DVDs; maps; and interactive media. National Geographic has funded more than 8,000 scientific research projects and supports an education program combating geographic illiteracy.

For more information, please call 1-800-NGS-LINE (647-5463)
Or write to the following address:
National Geographic Society
1145 17th Street N.W.
Washington, D.C. 20036-4688
U.S.A.

Visit us online at www.nationalgeographic.com/books

Printed in China

A MAZE ADVENTURE

Search for Pirate Treasure

Graham White

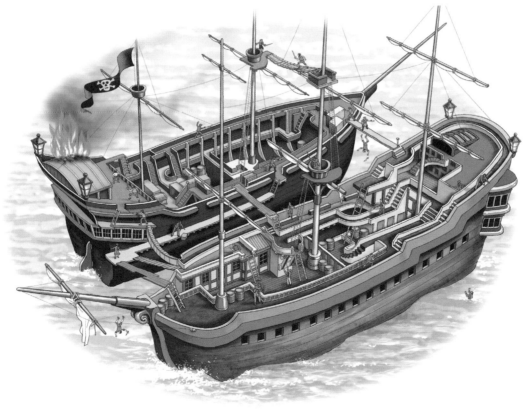

NATIONAL
GEOGRAPHIC

Washington, D.C.

While taking every care to check the facts presented in this book and the validity of the drawings, the publishers have allowed a certain amount of "artistic license" to enable the artist to create the mazes and tell a story. This has involved, for example, the inclusion of staircases and ladders to provide the routes and spaces needed for the mazes. The story and the coded puzzle are entirely fictional.

To complete the mazes, follow the clearly defined paths. You may go up and down stairs and ladders, etc., but no hopping over low walls or other obstructions that might look easy to climb over. The numbers next to certain pictures throughout the book are needed to crack the code on page 25.

Contents

Welcome to Life on the High Seas!

Hello, my name is Tom. I'm 12 years old. I live in a small village not far from a bustling coastal town where the people are kept busy with occupations mostly connected with the sea. In addition to fishermen, there are merchants and small traders who buy and sell all kinds of things from lands far away. Many people in the town are employed helping to build the mighty galleons that ply the oceans, trading with distant lands and fighting off pirate attacks.

My father is a sailor, and often returns home with tales of treachery, mutiny, and robbery on the high seas by pirates. These villains are a menace to ordinary, hardworking, honest seafarers. On my father's last voyage, pirates attacked the ship and took everything. Now our family is facing poverty because there wasn't a single coin left to pay the few crewmen, who barely escaped with their lives.

But all is not lost. I've heard tell of a ship being made ready to go in search of the pirates, with the task of regaining our lost treasure. It is a ship that I plan to be on!

Will you come with me? You will? That's great! Perhaps together we can help bring the evil pirates to justice, and also prevent my family from falling into the depths of poverty.

My father has taught me much about life at sea, and has taken me on board when his ship has been docked. I'll explain everything as we go. But we must first head for the town where the ship is being prepared for this great mission. So turn the page and we'll begin our adventure!

Maze 1. To the Coast

The coast isn't too far away, but just look at all those pathways! All of them will lead us to the port eventually, but there is only one short route. I hope we find it, because time is valuable. The ship will be leaving at high tide.

We have a good view of the sea from up here. It covers more than 70 percent of the Earth's surface. There are 2 tides in every 24 hours. The incoming tide is called the flood tide and the outgoing tide is called the ebb. Our ship will set sail when the sea level is at its highest, to leave on the ebb tide.

The countryside has many woods and forests. Trees are farmed much like any other crop, with new ones replanted to replace felled ones. Oak trees are used to build our mighty ships because oak is strong and doesn't rot easily. We also sometimes use elm for the keel, because that lasts a long time when kept in water. For some ships, spruce is imported for the tall masts.

Our journey to the coast is more difficult because I cannot read the road signs. Only the sons of gentlemen go to school. Royalty are taught by tutors who visit them at home. Don't worry, the ship's officers will be able to read the maps, so we shouldn't get lost!

Traveling overland is slow and hard work. We use packhorses and carts for transporting goods around. Messengers use fine horses for delivering important letters. Travel is dangerous though—there are many robbers waiting to pounce.

I'm glad you came along to help, otherwise I would have been wandering around the countryside forever! At last we have found our way, so let's turn the page and we'll continue through the town to find our ship.

Start

Finish

Start

I can see the ship in the harbor, but it is on the other side of the town. There are many streets and alleyways that could lead us in circles, so we must try not to lose our way.

This town is like most others—dirty! The streets are cobbled with pebbles or just earth, which of course gets muddy when it rains. People throw their garbage into the street, which encourages rats and other vermin. Rich merchants have homes built of stone, but most houses are wooden-framed, with wattle and daub panels.

5

There are many trades in the town, but here, most are shipwrights who build and repair our ships. Each trade has its own guild, which fixes wages and standards of workmanship with its members. I want to be an apprentice furniture maker. After seven years I will make a special piece, and, if it is good enough, I can join the guild myself. Perhaps one day I'll become an important person.

Ships are built and repaired in a special dry dock. Seaweed and barnacles are removed from the underside of ships—this is called "careening." The hulls are made watertight by "caulking" them—that is, sealing the gaps with "oakum," a mixture of horsehair and tar. A new ship can cost as much as $1,000.

Pirates often raid coastal towns for supplies, and have been here before. They are so ruthless, there is little the townsfolk can do to stop them. They celebrate being ashore by getting very drunk. They are not the sort of people who worry about tomorrow.

We've made it! Now we'll have to devise a way to get on board the ship without being noticed. So turn the page and we'll get a closer look at the loading dock.

Finish

Everyone is still very busy loading up the ship with all the provisions. These chests and boxes will give us plenty of places to hide, so we stand a good chance of going unnoticed while we take a rest.

Pirates prefer small, speedy ships such as two-masted schooners, so they can attack and escape quickly. Our ship is bigger, with larger sails and more powerful weapons. We should easily outgun them. I hope we reach them before they have a chance to spend all our money.

The supplies must be loaded carefully so that the weight is distributed evenly inside the ship to prevent her leaning over. There are lots of barrels of salted beef and fish. Sides of pork are salted and hung up to dry. The fish will be cut up and boiled into a

stew. Ship's biscuits are always baked twice, making the[m] so hard they are impossible to eat before softening w[ith] gravy or soup.

22

Most milk available doesn't keep well, so it is made into cheese. Water from the town is also not safe to drink so the sailors mostly drink beer. It is stockpile[d] on board in huge quantities. It is a good source of vitamin B, and also keeps the sailors happy!

The officers have plates and tankards made from a metal called pewter, which is a mixture of tin and lead. Knives, spoons, and flasks for carrying drinks are made from pewter too. Ordinary sailors use wooden implements, and their flasks are made from leather sealed with tar.

Why don't we carry some cargo to the ship, pretending we are hired helpers? We have to be quick. The longer we wander around, the greater our chances are of being caught.

Start

Start

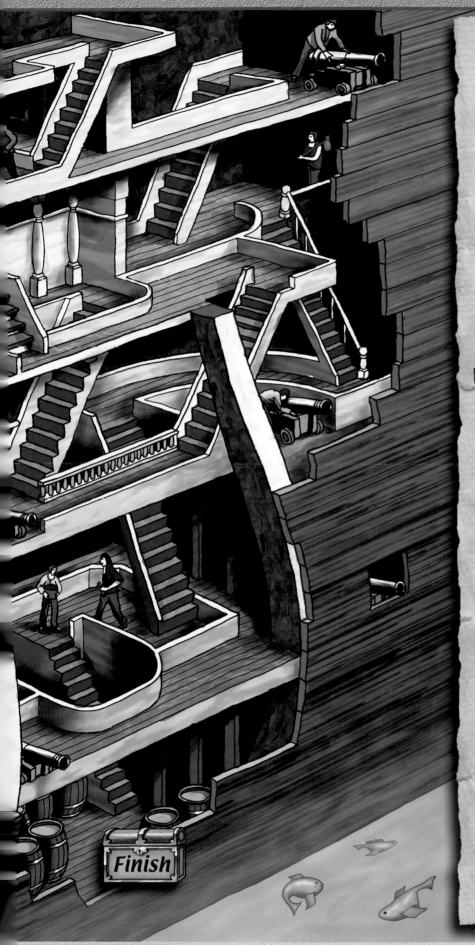

Finish

Yes! I've waited for this moment. At last we are on board the ship and on our way. We must find somewhere to hide. I think down belowdecks is the best place. There will be food and drink stored there too.

My father said that it could be horrible on board a ship, but I didn't expect this! It's very dark and everywhere is filthy, and there's an awful smell of bilge water and mildewed sails. Ugh! I can hear rats scratching, too.

We entered the ship on the forecastle deck. This is an upper deck in the front half of the ship. Below this are the gun decks, where sailors also put up their hammocks for sleeping. The officers have their cabins toward the rear, or "stern," of the ship, and spend much of their time on the "poop" and "quarter" decks there. Still below us are the "orlop" deck and the "hold," where we can hide.

This is the "galley," or ship's kitchen. The ship's cook has no easy task feeding a crew of several hundred hungry sailors. The ovens are made of brick to contain the heat, and have large copper pans above them for cooking in. Bellows are used to keep the ovens hot, and logs are stored here for fuel.

On the orlop deck is the ship's carpenter. He has a very important job—maintaining the wooden ship at all times. He must keep the decks waterproof and quickly plug any holes made by cannonballs during battle. He uses an adze for smoothing timbers, axes for chopping and trimming, and a brace and bit for drilling holes.

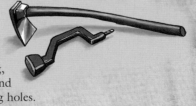

Watch your step; it gets quite dark down in the depths of the ship, and it's difficult to see where we're going. But at least that will help us to hide!

Oh dear, it seems we didn't find a dark enough corner after all—we have been discovered! But the ship has no cabin boys, so instead of punishment we have been set to work on deck.

The sailors become very skillful at tying lots of different knots for quickness and strength. They can fix sails and ropes that are damaged by storms or battle. Older sailors seem to possess almost magical skills.

10

They can predict the weather by the haze in the sky or a change of smell in the air. And they are able to locate spots in the open sea by contours of the seabed and patterns of currents.

Being a seafarer is one of the most dangerous of occupations. Sailors are very superstitious and wear lucky charms to protect them from the spirits of the sea. They would never carry an umbrella aboard ship, and wouldn't dream of changing a ship's name.

The rope-ladders up the masts are known as "ratlines." The sailors become very good at climbing these quickly. They learn to run along the yardarms (crosswise beams on masts) while the ship is moving. There are no safety nets, so one slip and they are finished! To let the sails down, they start from the outermost ends of the yardarm and work inward. This prevents the sail from filling with wind too quickly.

There are always two men who keep watch from the "crow's nest," a platform high in the mast. While a lookout is working, his mate sleeps in his bed until the end of the watch. Then they swap places—and fleas!

The lookout is jumping up and down—perhaps the ship's rats have climbed the mast! But wait, he has spotted the pirates! We must make sure th captain knows.*

Start

Finish

Our ship has caught up with the pirates, so let battle commence! While all the fighting is going on, we could sneak onto the pirate ship and see if they have our treasure on board.

Small ships and large crews mean cramped conditions for pirates. They need large numbers to gain an advantage when attacking larger ships. But often, their aggressive manner is enough on its own to bring about a quick surrender. Unruly crews are kept under control by rules laid down by the captain.

Anyone breaking the rules can expect some fearful punishments. Some are flogged, and others are "keel-hauled"—dragged under the ship by a rope. If the victim doesn't drown, his skin is cut by razor-sharp shells. Another cruel fate is to be hung over the sea in a basket and given a knife. The victim has the choice of dying of thirst or cutting the rope and drowning.

8

Pirates will go to great lengths to trick unsuspecting ships. Some have been known to dress up as ladies and pretend to be in distress. Pirates often fly friendly flags, only to change them at the last minute to the "Jolly Roger," the pirate flag.

Famous pirates whose names strike terror into the hearts of all decent seafarers are Blackbeard (below), Henry Morgan, William Kidd, and Bartholomew Roberts. But there are female pirates too—such as Mary Read and Anne Bonny—who fight as fearlessly as any man. Each pirate has his own version of the Jolly Roger, but flying a red one means that no mercy will be shown.

Our treasure isn't here, but I found a map in the pirate captain's cabin. It seems they have managed to hide it all on an island for safekeeping. We must make our way back to our ship. The captain will be very interested to see this!

St

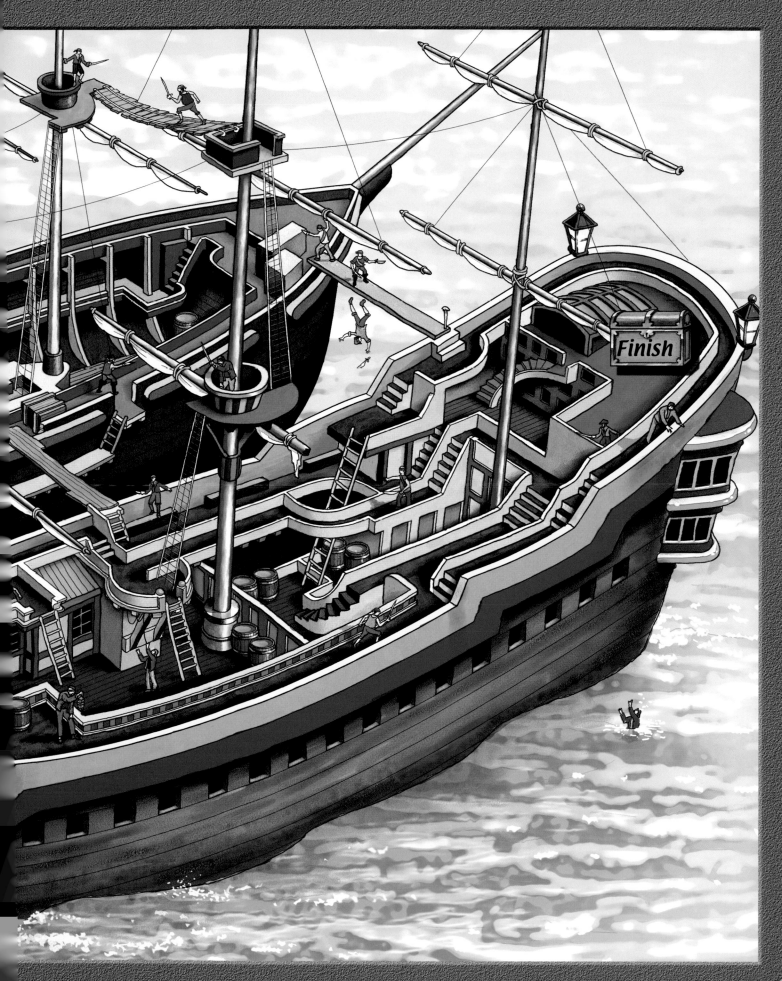

Finish

The battle has been fierce, but the pirates are defeated! We must now help care for our wounded sailors, who are belowdecks. We need to get to the medical supplies room as quickly as possible to lend a hand.

Another important member of the crew is the barber-surgeon, who deals with illness, disease, and the inevitable accidents onboard ship, along with injuries of battle. When not conducting his medical duties, he shaves the crew and cuts their hair. In all, he's a very busy man!

The barber-surgeon keeps all his instruments safe in a chest, along with medicine jars and ointments. He also keeps a saw handy for amputating arms and legs. If you were unfortunate enough to need this treatment, you would have to get very drunk first!

There are always casualties to attend to. Sailors, despite their skills, often fall from the rigging. Disease is rife, especially scurvy, which is caused by a lack of fruit in the diet. Seasickness is a common problem, and braw break out because of boredom. In fact, life ca be so hazardous that many sailors don't even bother to learn to swim—they believe that if yc fall into the sea, you are as good as dead anywa

We have captured some pirates and are taking them back with us to be brought to trial. If they are found guilty, they can expect to "dance the hempen jig"—the pirate term for hanging. The most notorious pirates will have their bodies hung up for all to see, and there they will stay until there is nothing left of them.

Our casualties are not too heavy, thank goodness. But we still need to get our treasure back. The captain has ordered the ship to set sail for the island shown on the map. I hope we can find where it's hidden.

Start

Finish

What a beautiful island! We are to go ashore with the landing party and help carry their equipment. It's very heavy, and these mountain paths are steep. But we must make camp before night falls.

The pilot is the navigator of the ship, keeping track of where we are. He has a small cabin toward the front of the ship with only his bed and a chest inside. He doesn't work here because, to navigate, he needs to be able to see the sun, the sea, and the stars to plot our position.

Captains usually like to keep close to land wherever possible. For longer journeys, they prefer to employ pilots who are familiar with the route. With no land visible, a good pilot can recognize an area by lowering a sounding lead overboard. This tells him the depth of water and type of seabed below.

14 The pilot has maps and charts. These are usually drawn on skins, which are resistant to damp conditions. But not all of the coasts have been recorded properly, so many maps are inaccurate.

The pilot also keeps a book with lists of landmarks, distances, dangerous rocks, and safe places to anchor.

19 The speed of the ship is measured using a "log reel." A wooden "chip" is thrown overboard attached to a line with knots tied in it at set intervals. As the ship moves away, the line is unreeled and the knots timed as they pass over the stern of the ship. This is the reason why speed at sea is recorded in "knots."

That was a long march, and it's hot here too. It's time for some food before we study the map to find exactly where the treasure is buried. Turn the page—I think we'll need your help with this!

Start

Cracking the Code

This is the treasure map we found on the pirate ship. The whereabouts of our treasure is marked on it, but the crafty pirates have made it difficult to find by writing the map in code.

We must fill in the missing letters on the blank panels at the bottom of the map. To do this we must travel around the island, starting on the southern shore, and follow the red route that is marked.

The first clue we come to is the sailor falling from the mast. If you look at the key on the left-hand side of the map, the same picture will tell you the letters to write in the first box. The next picture of the rat will give you the second box letters and so on. When you have been all around the island, you will end up with a sentence (without spaces between the words) that tells you exactly where the treasure is.

Unfortunately though, some of the pictures are missing. The pirates have just put a number instead. To find out which picture should be in its place, you will have to search carefully through the pages of this book, looking at the parchments on each maze. You will notice that some of the small pictures have a number next to them. These are the ones that should be on the map.

Remember, we can't turn the page to Maze 9 and make our way home until we have discovered the whereabouts of our treasure.

Good luck!

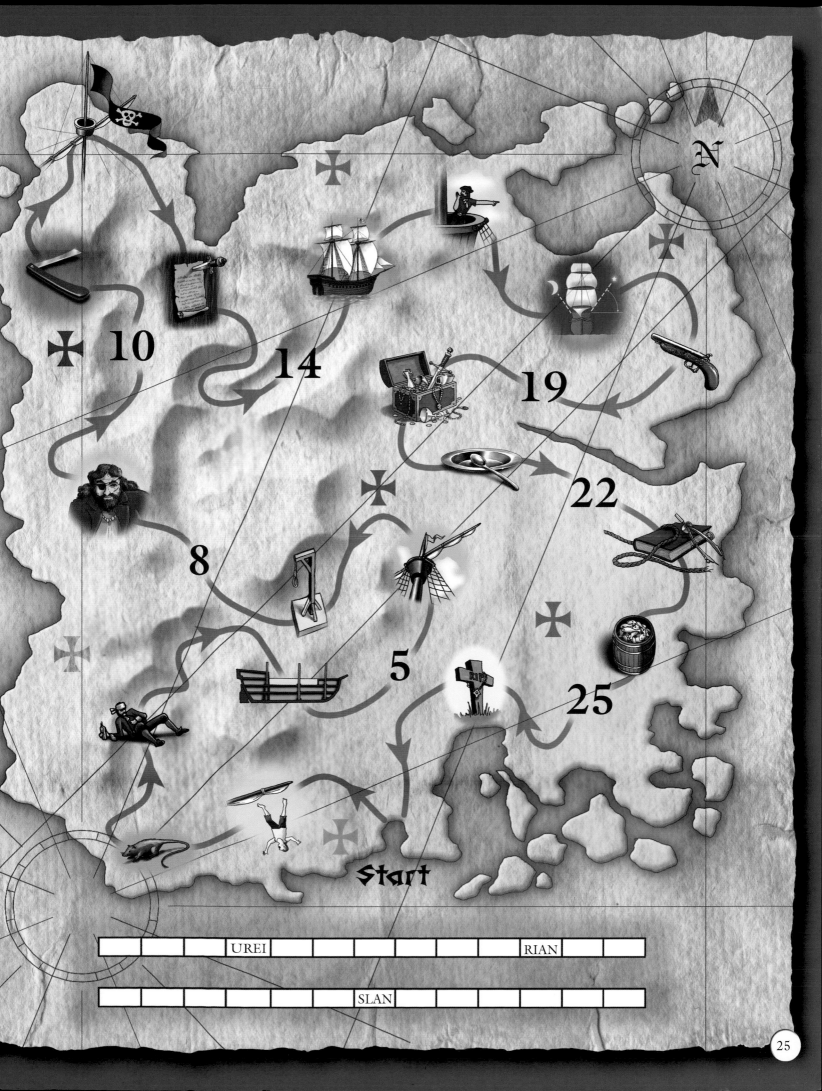

N

10

14

19

8

22

5

25

Start

| | | | UREI | | | | | | RIAN | |

| | | | | | SLAN | | | | | | | |

Maze 9. The Voyage Home

We've done it! We've found the treasure! We need to negotiate some islands and sandbanks safely, and we'll be home. My father will be happy that the pirates will pay for their crimes.

The main reason for piracy is, of course, to become very wealthy. And most pirates do—until they squander it while ashore. Their riches include gold, silver, coins, pearls, and jewels. Sometimes they take rare and useful commodities—spices, sugar, and medicinal drugs such as quinine, even silk from as far away as India and China.

Pirates take anything that is useful or of value—things such as weapons, ammunition, food, barrels of rum and beer, rope, sails, tools, anchors, books, documents, and scientific instruments. A treasured prize is a ship's medical chest.

The pirate code states the rules for splitting the plunder. Usually, it is six shares for the captain, two for the first mate, and one each for every crewman. Some treasures are difficult to share out evenly though, and some fierce fights have broken out between crewmen.

25

Choosing the right ship with the right cargo to attack is always a problem for the pirate captain. Because the spoils are shared out among the crew, he risks a mutiny if they fight for little, or if he chooses not to attack at all. The Spanish Main (northern coast of South America) has become a popular hunting ground for pirates because of the Spanish treasure ships that frequent the area.

The treasure will now be returned, and my father will be paid. We have also been rewarded for our bravery. Thanks to your help, our family will no longer be poor. And the high seas will be a safer place!

Finish

Start

Solutions

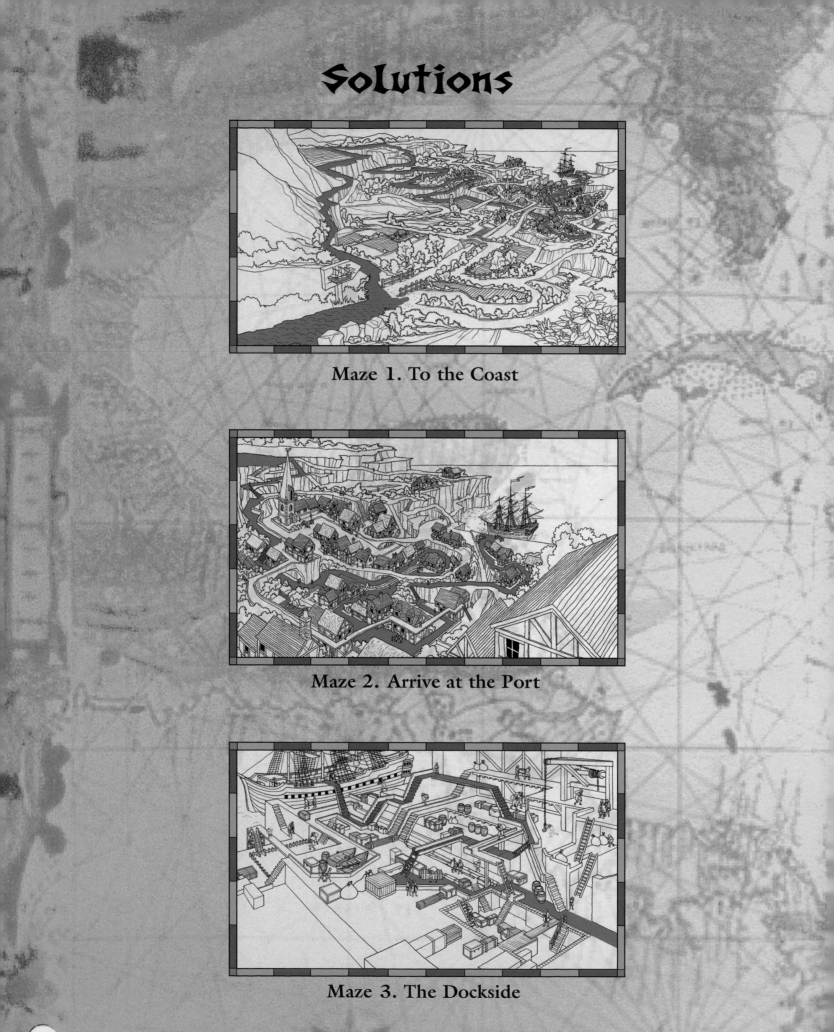

Maze 1. To the Coast

Maze 2. Arrive at the Port

Maze 3. The Dockside

Maze 4. Belowdecks

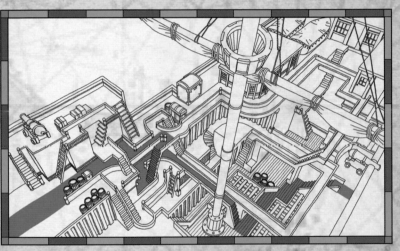

Maze 5. Upper Decks

Maze 6. The Sea Battle

Maze 7. The Wounded

Maze 8. Buried Treasure

The hidden treasure is buried beneath a rock that is triangular shaped. It is near to the center of the island where the blue cross is drawn.

The code cracked (use a mirror!)

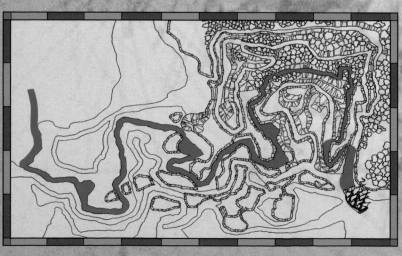

Maze 9. The Voyage Home

Glossary of Terms

adze
A heavy tool with a curved blade used for cutting or shaping large pieces of wood.

barnacles
Small shellfish that attach themselves to objects under water, such as rocks and bottoms of ships.

bilge water
Dirty water that collects in the bilge, or bottom area, of a ship.

cabin boy
A boy or young man who works as a servant on a ship.

careening
The process of removing barnacles and other debris from the underside of a ship.

caulking
To seal the underside of a ship to make it watertight.

crow's nest
A platform at the top of a ship's mast, from where a seafarer can get the best view of distant objects.

dry dock
An enclosed part of a port, from which the water can be removed, for building or repairing ships.

forecastle deck
An upper deck toward the front of a ship.

galleon
A large sailing ship used between the 1600s and 1800s.

hold
The part of a ship where the goods being carried are stored.

hull
The main bottom part of a ship that goes into the water.

keel-hauling
Punishing a sailor by dragging him by a rope from one side of a ship underneath the hull to the other side of the ship.

log reel
A device used by sailors to determine the speed at which the ship was traveling.

mutiny
The act of sailors refusing to obey the orders of those in authority, such as the captain and his officers.

oakum
A mixture of horsehair and tar used to seal the underside of a ship.

pilot
The navigator of the ship, who uses the sun, the sea, and the stars to determine the ship's whereabouts.

plunder
Things that have been stolen, usually after a battle.

poop deck
The raised part at the back of a ship.

quarter deck
Part of the upper level of a ship, at the stern, or back, which is used mainly by officers.

ratlines
The name given to the rope ladders used to climb the masts.

rigging
The ropes that support the mast and sails of a ship.

scurvy
A disease caused by a lack of vitamin C from not eating enough fruit and vegetables.

shipwright
A craftsman employed in the process of building ships.

Spanish Main
A name given to the stretch of water along the north coast of South America.

stern
The back end of a ship or boat.

wattle and daub
The name given to a type of walling used in the construction of buildings. It was made by interweaving rods and branches (wattle), and plastering them together with a paste (daub).

Index